literally show me a healthy person

Tyrant Books

Tyrant Books
827 N Lamar Blvd
Oxford, MS 38655

www.NYTyrant.com

ISBN 13: 978-0-9992186-0-0

Cover design by the author
Book design by Adam Robinson

10 9 8 7

literally show me a healthy person

Darcie Wilder

Tyrant Books
New York, Rome

in third grade when everyone cool had glasses like arthur from arthur i faked having bad eyesight at the eye doctor's but i wanted to be sure that they thought my eyes were bad enough to need glasses so i said i couldn't see colors and they stopped the test and i had to wait in the waiting room and my mom went to cry in the bathroom and they guilted me into confessing the truth and i had to retake the whole test and then they dilated my pupils so i really couldnt see and it was so scary and they gave me fake glasses that i was too ashamed to ever actually wear and now my mom is dead and i have astigmatisms

grammar question: do you wake up "with terror" or "in terror"?

in rehab we did a meditation we lied down on the floor and closed our eyes and our shrink said we walked around a pond until we found a kid sitting on a bench and we talk to the kid and we take the kid around the pond and how is the kid and my kid was limping from a gash on her foot and our shrink said this was our inner child

what if banks was yahe mommy and you have to vosit and say i love you and then have to one day bury

once my dad bought me a plastic bill clinton mask that covered my whole eight year old head it was heavy plastic with no ventilation and i couldn't breathe and would cut my neck sometimes but i put it on and wore a suit on halloween and went as bill clinton and whenever anyone opened their doors they would laugh or were horrified but i didn't understand i was eight and no one told me what the lewinsky scandal was or that it happened that year

that picture of the dead rat on instagram w caption 'i just crushed its skull' - the guy who posted that photo - i had sex with that guy

plan b is kind of a party drug

friday night imagining everyone i know dying

starring at the wall thats fucking my wall im starring at my wal

people moving to Los Angeles is my least favorite thing i can think of besides me being homeless or my family dying

i guess what im saying is single people aint tickled enough, maybe integrate tickling into the office more

whenever my dad would drive me and my brother up the fdr he would point at the water under the bridges and tell us to never go swimming there because there are cyclones under the bridges and we'd die. he also, when we were crossing the bridge into marble hill, told us to never cut our tongues off because they don't grow back

godiva is my least favorite regular spam email i went there once to get my grandma a nice birthday gift today is her birthday again and i missed her call because i am playing music from my phone in the salon today but when i bought her chocolates the guy behind the counter asked if i wanted to be put on the mailing list and get a free piece of chocolate and i specifically asked i remember very vividly asking if they would do this and they said no so i said my email at gmail dot com and i picked whatever disappointing chocolate that i didnt enjoy and then pretty soon afterward i got godiva emails every single morning at 9:18 am and sometimes it says it's sent from piper, which is a name of a kid i babysit so i'll think she's emailing me and i'll get super excited and i'll even open it and it's not her it'll be this chocolate peddler. ive unsubscribed several times and marked as spam even more but i still get messages

1 cat = 14 rats

in film school i opened my netflix on a projector and it recommended MOTHER-DAUGHTER TEARJERK-ERS FROM THE 1980s in front of everyone

crazy girls are just quirky girls who've maybe seen their parents try to kill each other one Tuesday morning i called my dad to say hi and i asked what he was doing and he said "buying life insurance. you're welcome"

when i was ten i helped a holocaust survivor in my building sell pottery every saturday morning on the corner and i would set up her table and break it down at the end of the day and one day there was a baby bird that was on the ground i didnt know what to do and thought that my mom would know what to do and she might come downstairs to visit so i didnt do anything but my mom never came and i was taking apart the table and i turned around and the bird was dead the bird's belly was flat and laid in a pool of its bird blood and intestines and heart i had stepped on the bird i killed the bird i told the old woman and she said "oh no," and laughed it off and now when i visit she doesn't recognize me in the hallway

steve did you ever love me

when i was young i played a game where i was plastic and delivered pizza and a game where i was real and died forging a river and a game where i lived in a house and swam in a pool with no exit

saying "awesome" on work phone calls is just another way to stay punk

on the first day of fifth grade my dad walked me to school and we stopped at a bodega that is now a store that sells dog collars and dog leashes since the bodega was shut down for selling the cigarettes to teenagers but

literally show me

it was maybe the year 2000 so it was still open and he brought me there and he bought me a twinkie and said to me in my face "when i was your age i would get a twinkie for lunch every day" i took this to mean "eat a twinkie for lunch every day to earn my love" and i tried but we couldn't leave the school for lunch every day so one day a week i would eat a twinkie for lunch and the next year we were allowed to leave school for lunch more often and i gained a lot of weight that year

i will do your taxes

one birthday i was on snack duty and convinced everyone we should buy six pounds of shrimp and a birthday cake. madeline made us buy two bags of pretzels we left unopened around the shrimp. emily said her mom only ate pretzels and when she pulled out the parking lot started projectile vomiting

seafood allergy

i angHave to be Pretyyty

i want everyone ive had sex with to fail

how come "put me out of my misery" only really means one thing

in dunkin donuts i asked dad if he knew we'd hang out again after he met me in the hospital after i was born and he said, "i think i had an idea but you know: i don't ask your brother about his relationships, i don't ask you about your relationships. but i want you to know that no matter what happens and what you do or don't do you won't turn into a pumpkin. i was 28 when i met your mother."

I'd be a bad wife but a good ghost

he said i already told him about killing the bird and we were having sex the first time too

im reading "27 people harry styles dated in 2013" the only phrases i'm letting myself be allowed to use this week are "no substitute for a mother's love" and "i cant even hear the noise anymore," alex asked me how long i thought i could go, dead, before people found out i said three or four days. he thought two months

two weeks after malt liquor monday the condom fell out

baby poodle backflipped/fell on his noggin and i laughed out loud and the man at the pooch and poodle shop gave me eyes like i the goofball!

not everyone has hair, teeth

list of my dad's advice: stand by the wall or someone will push you on the tracks, never cut off your tongue, if you fall on the rink make a fist or ice skates will cut off your fingers, avenues go north/south, never stay in a relationship for the sex, never cook bacon naked, never make a right turn going over ten mph, only say that stuff behind their back, don't touch the third rail, drugs and alcohol just slow you down, put bacon fat in old cans in the freezer, never get married because you think it's something you should do, and, at the hospice ATM emptying my mom's bank account: more than one way to skin a cat

yall hear that everything on the internet will be deleted thursday? fucked up, right

when we leave the hospice we walk down eastchester ave and mary picks up a penny and puts it in her pocket and says she tapes them in a notebook with where and when she found them.

on the second anniversary dad takes me to the church on pine street and mary sits in the next pew and does a reading for the service and i don't listen and my throat gets tight and they read mom's name and i don't listen and mary walks me to the electronic candles with no flame and gives me a quarter and i slide the quarter in the slot and she takes my hand and holds her hand over my hand and presses down on the candle button until the lightbulb flicks on and she closes her eyes and says, "this is for everything we learned from them. everything they did or didn't mean to teach us."

in the movie midnight cowboy dustin hoffman dies on a bus. in the movie the graduate dustin hoffman dies on a bus. in the movie i heart huckabees dustin hoffman never takes the bus

how much does money cost

u can be over him and still want to ruin his life. multitudes danny pushed me into the trash bags on the street when belinda babysat and sat me down in the closet, opened a marble bound composition book and showed me the multiplication tables

dad keeps handing me printed copies of his will when we meet for dinner

on second avenue and fourteenth an eleven year old pointed at me and shouted, "she has a sad love story"

my roommate said hunter is dating someone "small and quiet. everything you're not"

during hurricane sandy i catfished my boyfriend and ate a fourteen egg omelet and he said you're fucking crazy never talk to me again and my shrink said, "far worse things happen every day." i'm ignoring the girl that pretends she never fucked my boyfriend senior year and that she didn't steal my halloween costume she wants to meet up while we're both wednesday addams

a four year old in the elevator asked his mom "when we talk do we think about what we say or just say it?"

we had a moment of silence at breakfast when bernie mac died. anthony kiedis held my hand

the boy in the elevator pointed at me said "you're scary" and got out at the next available floor

population control via only building buildings less than eleven stories. oh you want kids, huh. where you gonna put em when i woke up the phone in the other room rang and i went online and told jasmine i wanted to go outside even though it was 2 AM and on my way to the kitchen dad called me over and sat me on the futon he slept on cause he couldn't sleep in his bed anymore and he said she's gone she died and what do i want to do now that your mom is dead so we walked down park terrace west and it started to snow and we sat in the coffee shop that's a fish market now

when you eat the bread and "you'll have to learn everything over again"

moving to la is a temporary solution to a permanent problem

i missed my flight sitting twenty feet from the gate because i didn't know the difference between boarding and departure

Plot Keywords: Oral Sex | Video | Intellectual | Art Gallery | Tattoo | See more»

"do you eat out of the garbage" is a question on the dating site i met my boyfriend on. two exes IM'd me at the same time and asked how my boyfriend they both can't remember the name of is

time to use the new toothbrush. i went to college and have a boyfriend. i can't wait until my boyfriend leaves so i can watch stepmom

should i break up with my boyfriend because he let me fall asleep in my make up. i slept in my make up every night for the first six weeks and he recorded me snoring on valentine's day.

i just want a boyfriend who tells me we are breaking up when we break up

when are we breaking up

i booked a ticket home to watch grandma die but it was my boyfriend's friend's birthday. after the party he said "no one thought you were weird but i think you think you were weird"

on the way to the car i tasted her cigarette on his lips

it started to snow when i woke up on heidi's couch to my boyfriend's texts of four molly pills and a dark video from a strip-club with the music blown out when dad called me and told me grandma died

before my birthday party my boyfriend watched me eat 12 wings and broke up with me. i asked if he wanted to pretend to still be together for the party. he said no

can i still call these "boyfriend jeans"

three days later we got back together and fucked with an expired marc jacobs condom

my boyfriend's friend and her boyfriend asked how dating my boyfriend is. i did wobbly hand motion

since then one of them killed themselves

in the car i took a picture of the sun on the dashboard

tombstone ideas
- later, nerds
- soon enough
- it's fine i'm just tired
- no

i'm moving three thousand miles away on tuesday. i asked my boyfriend to call out of work for my last day. he said no. it's an unpaid internship

on our first date we got drunk at an in-n-out and he blacked out during out first kiss

even cowgirls get suicidal

i dreamt everyone died

a boy called me ugly in a dream

i was on this rooftop coming down

and showed geoff the skyline

i remember telling him he had the perfect dick and then he said when i was on molly i just said the worst things i had ever done

we were in bushwick

i never cried during sex before

his dick was ok

i wonder if i'll ever talk to geoff again

his new girlfriend updated her vlog

i tried to invite geoff to pinterest but it didn't let me because he blocked me on facebook

once i was with geoff and we were taking separate cars to my house and on the way i stopped and secretly ate a double bacon cheeseburger

i never fucked in front of an urn before

he came where grandma died

he said i love you and it made sense.

i got an iud and we had sex and went to dave & busters and went on the motorcycle ride and his cum dripped out thru my tights on the plastic motorcycle

im going to make the same mistakes as last night but louder

my boss said, "you have a future. but it looks a lot like your past"

sometimes i put my car in drive but it doesn't unlock from neutral and it's like: i already have enough metaphors for my life

los angeles is actually designed solely for people to lose their money, the highest brow pyramid scheme

forever 21 smells like sand

today i declined invitations to a kombucha brewing party in New York and a vision board party in Los

Angeles. i wish people referred to cucumbers like they do butterflies. it the same metaphor.

where can i get nike dunks?

alright yall ready to die

i miss my ex's friend Beto who doesn't know how to tie his shoes.

hunter held my hand and tried to fuck again

sometimes when people introduce themselves to me or ask me how i am i can't think of anything to say or do except show them my tongue and sometimes try to bite them, but i only bite if i've met them before. i was wearing red lipstick the night wreck room closed. mark thought it was blood I laid on the sidewalk for a phone call and peed in the stairway

i heard the basement of wreck room was haunted

my boyfriend used to reassure me that im "good crazy" until one day he suddenly stopped.

my shrink said i could be ok one day and i asked what he says to everyone else

he said, "i say, 'it's going to take a lot of work.'"

then i told him about getting hit by car

my earthquake survival kit is dying

when i was eleven my dad got me out of bed by saying, "there's breakfast in the kitchen with your name on it" and when i got up there was an entenmann's powdered donut with "DAR" scratched into it.

A NICE WOMAN SHOT LASERS INTO MY HAND TODAY

once my boyfriend was subconsciously ignoring me so much that he asked me "does darcie" instead of "do you"

his friend beto made a playlist in the car called 'death grips'

beto teaches zumba now

ive had sex less intimate than the silent toe corn shaving with my podiatrist

i was playing in one of the wheelchairs in the lobby when i heard the speakers say code blue on the tenth floor next to a thirty-person family sitting in the waiting room chairs outside the ICU and the doctor came out to speak to them and they started wailing and crying and hugging right when dad walked in through the automatic sliding doors and he didn't notice so we got in the elevator and got to mom's room just as they were running in for the code blue and someone yelled, "get her daughter out of the room" and they took me and told me she doesn't have a pulse anymore it's a heart attack and the social worker squeezed my hand and asked if knew what that means

people i forget died: paul walker, brittany murphy, heath ledger, steve irwin, greg giraldo, paul blart, james gandolfini, philip seymour hoffman, adrienne shelly, brad renfro, robin williams, ryan dunn

Keeping my hand elevated

if we all meet up in the afterlife aren't murder-suicides more like a life sentence?

my borderline mother died: can't live with her, can't live without her

i never told my mom i got my period, she just opened my dresser and found a year's worth of blood-stained underwear. my shrink thinks my mom lied about finding a year's worth of blood-stained underwear because i told her i didn't keep a year's worth of blood-stained underwear in my dresser drawer

tell me how you can suck someone's dick but can't replace your mother's love?

valentine's day tip: if the store says "open" it means they have to talk to you

i just realized that i, too, can be young dumb and full of cum

i have a septum ring so they already know i give good head

i have six hospice room phone contacts saved as "mom"

i asked my dad "how did you propose to mom" and he said "i already answered this: i don't remember" my mom sat me down and told me sex was just like the blink-182 song "feeling this"

alex and jamie lived above irving street where we got a thirty-rack of bud in my vest with the pbr back patch and alex said "darcie get a blink-182 tattoo" so i put on the song "dumpweed" that goes "she's a fucking nightmare unpredictable it's hard for me to stay here i need a girl that i can train" and alex got a needle and traced "nightmare" above my elbow but he started poking me and dipping the needle into ink and poking me but he didn't leave enough room so i woke up with a misspelled blink-182 tattoo

whenever i start wondering if im gay i put on The L Word

i said i heard purple is a healing color and she said the elephant removes obstacles, brings abundance and protects while she wrapped the bracelet around my wrist and looped the end into the elephant trunk charm she said the trunk needs to face towards you at all times and that because it was from her and because it was from my uncle their energy together was protecting me and then my uncle never paid her and she stopped replying to my texts

my uncle said my mom shot a man in cleveland i asked if he survived he said "i think it was curtains for him"

my mother, the killer

my uncle adopted and gave away six dogs before i turned eighteen when i turned twenty-one he let me pick out a dog he said he'd have it for a year until i graduated and then it would be mine when the dog arrived he had it for a week and then his ex-boyfriend put it in his carry-on and took him to los angeles without asking me and allie told me to meet her at the free yoga class on eighth street the room was completely full there was no room and i was wearing size B l'eggs control top sheer black tights and the lady told us to go into pigeon pose our one leg was crossed over our other leg and we folded over and i started to cry and couldn't stop crying the whole rest of class while people looked so i tried to stop but my nose was running and the snot was wet and cold and chafing the skin above my lips it was so red and i had to wipe it on my arm and everyone in the room was quieter and not crying and fifty pounds skinnier than me and after allie and i got tea and i went home and my uncle's ex-boyfriend still has my fucking dog

mom used to say my uncle did crack in the apartment across the hall and when she died my uncle said he hated living there cause she kept trying to catch him smoking crack

my uncle got off with "assault with a deadly weapon" instead of attempted murder

should i do mushrooms in the room where my grandma died

geoff and his brother and i did shots of tequila on houston where i met paul three years later with his bike that said "crest toothpaste" and six months before that where i dropped joe's bottle of poppers. geoff and his brother and i took a shot of black velvet whiskey every time she sings the words 'black velvet' in the song 'black velvet' the next day i threw up at work. geoff and his brother and i spent $53 at taco bell before i got in a fight with a cab driver. he made me pay $8 and i left his door open. geoff did 'lovefool' at karaoke and i knew then that he didn't really love me

how many people did you guys's mom kill

geoff's parents didn't ask me any questions . just because geoff doesn't think im funny doesn't mean im not funny

dad called mom "a total bitch" for something she said on her deathbed about white castle jalapeno cheeseburgers

another intern invited me to her party and we drove and parked and walked to the door but turned around and drove home and parked and drank in his car. i spilled $1 malt liquor in the front seat the night before he drove his boss to the airport

today is a new day!

geoff said we had to get the $35 volcano blast for three to four people they put it on the table it was on fire geoff told me not to take a picture but i took a picture and we took pictures in the photobooth it was his last night on the first night i met him we got drunk at an in-and-out because i forgot my id and he drove me home on our second date i met him at the short stop and he kissed me in the photobooth and a few months later told me he didn't remember it the picture is taped to my kitchen doorframe when we left otto's i showed him stuytown where my uncle lived when i was a kid and where my dad lived as a kid and where he was climbing a fence when he was ten and he got caught on the spike and his arm ripped open and his uncle went to get his mom from food emporium and dad walked to the hospital cause no one in the park helped him then geoff and i took the bus uptown and we went too far we went to the UN and we had to get a cab and i went to lay in the bed in the room where my grandma died and i opened his phone and opened a text and in the text there was a screenshot of his tinder profile and i asked if he was ever on tinder and he said no and then i went to the bathroom and threw up and started shaking on the bathroom floor and kept on throwing up and said im so sorry and he said it's ok i don't care and it's time for him to go to jfk and i said you have an hour if you take a cab so i paid and we laid for an hour and in the cab we were still drunk and the sun was coming up and he was wearing his yellow hoodie his favorite color i painted my nails yellow for him but i smudged the polish when they were still wet and i never fixed it the whole two weeks i took a picture of him in the terminal when he didn't want me to and then i left for my uncle's and fed his dogs and laid in his bed and when geoff got home he sent me a picture in the mirror that we used to wake up next to it had only been seven hours but he was gone

he blocked my number

i asked my dad what he did at 2pm the day i was born. he said, "i was at the recovery room. it was a bar a few blocks away from the hospital"

it's january ninth and so far this year two people died in the electrical fire across the street and a teacher at my high school set a kid on fire and my friend's landlord was kidnapped and set on fire in a dumpster

stay away from leos!! aries, and sagittarius

i'm cancer rising, bitch

cant wait till assisted suicide is legal. we're gonna wild out and replace our blood with hi-c

last night there was a murder-suicide on my block. a man killed himself and his pregnant girlfriend in a hotel for people with aids.

the neighbor said "i've just seen so much"

i pass the hotel on my way to work and once when mark slept over. mark and i hooked up because our moms are dead

in tarkovsky's nostalghia he lights and holds a candle and walks from one side to the other without it going out

my math tutor died of aids i remember he loved his golden retriever and buying crack cocaine in fort tryon park. i loved the simpsons game for xbox

i can't cum the first time and i only have one night stands. how many rotisserie chickens am i supposed to eat in one night. how do you know it's going to be a one night stand

liz cried all new years eve so i told her her and david would probably get back together and that i brought my tinder match she fucked to the last ever party on avenue a and he put on black rob's "like whoa" and someone put on the stove and heated up a ring and tried to brand this guy's hand and the skin on his hand instantly dissolved and swole up so fast and it smelled like burning flesh so he took me to a goth bar and i don't remember anything except sucking his dick in the bathroom and when we came back out we didn't get kicked out but the bouncer stood over me staring until we left and i hailed a cab for home and he got in and said he felt bad and i don't remember anything besides telling him everything is fine and then next thing i remember is when i came to we were fucking and he said he had to leave because he was sad

when mom and i fought we used to start the day over

when i was 18 my dad gave me a bootleg copy of he's just not that into you but i lost the dvd and when i gave the empty case to hunter he said "i don't get it"

we had sort of a will-they-won't-they except with who gave who the scabies

wake up in the morning turn over and ask:
is this as bad for you as it is for me

i wish my face was in a pile of cold dirt in a good way

the man at duane reade called me a witch and then i ate a bag of mushrooms

on mushrooms in the room where my grandma died sam did a line and asked if it was coke or heroin and gian showed us a video of the most pain known to man. they're called suicide headaches because everyone kills themselves. there's no cure. the man in the video was screaming until they brought him an oxygen tank. gian said the oxygen doesn't help him. nothing does

i washed my feet in the tub and realized when i die everything that ever happened to me dies

i laid in bed where my grandma died and tried to sleep

gian said "is she ok?" and they said yes

sometimes i wake up and my body can't move

when i die please dont embalm me i know new york state laws require embalming but when i die please listen please dont embalm me i know there are new york state laws about preservation and transport of body but please forgo embalming please just put me in the ground where i become a tree or a fern or a pile of dust and everyone can eulogize me except hunter

dad dont embalm me

i'm the only one in this diner at 4:30 AM not wearing a neon vest that says "waste solutions" and i don't remember the plane but i remember going to lax with grandma january 2013 thinking it was the last time i'd see her and taking public transportation back to echo park i remember eating french fries in the in-and-out parking lot with a dead battery waiting for AAA listening to "red nose" and i hadn't seen geoff yet geoff was at work i was seeing ashley, geoff broke up with me two days before right after i'd got my misspelled "nightmare" tattoo covered up

i drank too much vodka and laid in geoff's bed after he talked about breaking up again and his friends asked if i was ok i wasn't ok he opened the door and asked if i was ok and i didn't say anything and he said she's ok and went back in the other room so i went to my car and laid in the back and felt the leather on my face it was cold and i heard them come out they shined their iphones into the backseats of all the cars until they found me

waht if we only had 1 tooth

yesterday i got drunk alone to angela's ashes. guess how many children die in that movie it's lit

do any rich ppl want to. or hot ppl

condoms for eye contact

i have a bad sense of smell so i'm always worried i smell like shit. i'm worried my tattoos remind people of the holocaust. i'm worried i look better in pictures and disappoint people on-site. i'm worried of "losing it all" and i'm worried about thinking i have anything to lose.

three weeks ago at the c-town check-out the cashier said "I want a hot dog" and we shared meaningful eye contact and laughed

a customer came in while my boss was popping my zit. my boss smiled through her teeth and said "don't move"

I dreamt about autocorrect last night

the awakening of the heart seminar was $600 and the co-star of a major 2000s sitcom stared into my eyes as i said i felt worthless and i said i didn't matter and she cried. we stood in a circle and hugged and everyone laughed at me

people laugh if you say something serious in the tone of something funny. if you say something funny in the tone of something serious they block your phone number

they said we would transform, not change

you gave someone your heart-shaped cubic zirconia pin for their heart-shaped cubic zirconia pin and then you exchanged that heart-shaped cubic zirconia pin for someone else's heart-shaped cubic zirconia pin and over and over again. the heart-shaped cubic zirconia pin represented our heart. this lady looked at me, looked at her heart-shaped cubic zirconia pin, shook her head 'no' and walked away.

they told us to find the person with the most inner beauty and touch them. the co-star of a major 2000s sitcom touched my shoulder so i touched her forearm. they

literally show me

said pick the person who has the most inner beauty but this time don't lie. i picked someone else

after the three-day $600 awakening of the heart seminar i went to sat's house and ate carrots and celery as her dog Dottie barked at me and i lost my heart-shaped cubic zirconia pin

Dottie licked my feet and laid next to my grandma while she slept on the couch. they're both dead now

crying eyes full heart still losing

the first time i ever drank andy took us back to our freshman year converted triple, poured a shot of whiskey and said, "you can do this, but you can't do this because of him"

of course it was about him

this famous dude's daughter gave us coke until this guy got a condom from the bodega at six am but i woke up to him fucking me raw and she woke up and kept saying "it's ok i don't care" over and over so i left and we never really talked again. later she texted to ask if i was ok

"empty yourself of everything. let your mind become still. ten thousand things rise and fall as the self"

i, for one, feel it's absolutely wild to see my dad move on from my mom to find the love of his life who hates everything i stand for

between the bathroom and my boyfriend i drank a whiskey sour in thirty seconds and texted jamie "i love you" and threw up in los globos' second floor bathroom just as geoff started getting a fever. after the show we sat on the curb and he wouldn't leave me or get the car so i took off my shirt and ran into traffic and the next day i threw up at work

the friend of the guy who gave me a concussion hit on me and when i turned him down he circulated screenshots of my private twitter account

so i guess im just gonna smash this like till i die

lately feel:
god grant me the serenity
young thug sounds happy
interests: hot sauce, sitcoms
i dont care about aliens
i kill houseplants to feel more powerful
can someone give me $500
does anyone like the band death grips
i like when kool ad sings "dont ask me what it means
    just kiss me"

does dirt die

how do i block everyone on this website. when i use emoticons like <3 and :(instead of emojis it means i mean it more. i guess what we learned is we don't have to love each other to use the same website. ryan defriended me because of the flamewar. i said it's not ok to say the word 'f*****' do u understand what i said without me having to say it. i can't say it.

how do u say it without saying it

i don't even know who my tweets are about anymore

since when is everyone better than Hilary Duff

i forgot i had a job interview until they wrote me that i didn't get it

it's more honest to smoke crack than cigarettes. i'm getting off birth control to have the upper hand. i'm shouting at windows like i'm in the movie kids. get out of the local band's way, their uber xl is pulling up.

i'm passing the guys smoking crack on 43rd right before the field trip does.

41st street always has the best garbage. the guy on 44th got his gangrene out. sometimes he changes his gauze when i walk by and there's no skin it's just red.

one of the guys from the gym says he lives across from the hess gas station and went to bed drunk when he woke up it was a sunoco. he said the guy living under the overpass left after the blizzard and when we walked passed his stuff i said i hope he's back soon and the guy said nothing

i forgot i had been drinking when i showed up

and drank like so much fucking wine

who cares

i dont care

leave me to fucking die, imo

accidentally searched "tit's fine"

on my work computer

what if my cat doesn't cum the first time

what do you do when a cat dies?

do you just throw out the cat.

i don't like what i named my cat so i just started calling her "my cat"

after my job interview sam asked why i wore a tshirt with Xs on the nipples.

i realized when the towers fell all those people died. Pull out my phone like here are my 24 favorite work-appropriate "9/11 was an inside job" tattoos.

A model's job is to be prettier than me

when i was young everyone seemed to say "it's ok if you're not your best friend's best friend" but now it's like fuck that

i heard dentists perform surgery on decapitated human heads

can i join your noise band

how come people only drug their kids at the dentist

i buried my mother but i still feel my strongest when im drunk but not texting exes. he hasn't texted back so im assuming my boyfriend hasn't checked his phone in 6 months

i live and work in times square (i think about isis a lot)

i got a job so high i have to take two elevators. this elevator smells like diaper once it smelled like vomit and once i smelled someone's cavity.

freaky friday: cathy and garfield switch bodies. cathy has to deal with humiliating litterbox conditions, garfield hates folgers coffee

whenever someone's mean to me at work i just rest assured once i slap on that $30 eyeliner i'll get that sweet hot validation after hours. i walked into times square sephora to buy eyebrow pomade and instead she took off all my makeup and called me beautiful

dad and i starring in a father-daughter buddy comedy where i throw out his food and he says he never loved my mother

im in the woods listening to my uncle flirt on speakerphone. he left his email up asking if his uncle murdered anybody. i fell asleep in my uncle's bed i woke up and he was hovering over me with a boxcutter

any bodies

any parties

eating a sandwich as my friend sam texts me pictures of dead bodies

he says, "you wouldn't believe the sound flesh makes hitting a bucket"

calling them 'catacombs' is just a fancy way to rationalize hoarding dead bodies

sorry i'm late it's just this girl called me fat in the sixth grade

i never thought id use my iud this little

something's in my hair

i hope this is cum in my hair

my ex's dog is trying to seduce me

im fat because my mom died

honestly it's kind of cheating if u need drugs or alcohol to ruin ur life

in college there was a night called zombie prom we all dressed as zombies and i wore the same outfit i wore every day but with more blood and walked down the main path and saw this guy with his arms around two girls and the girls yelled "darcie" and the guy yelled "who the fuck is darcie"

this girl defriended me just because i slept with her boyfriend a measly 6 times five years ago

my last boyfriend joined tinder before the break up.

none of my boyfriends ever liked my art. my last boyfriend said his ideal girl would be really short and extremely dumb. i dyed my hair red for him

jamie handed me old overhold and i took five gulps and the boy i liked who hated me was already at the apartment and i kept drinking and everyone left my birthday party i went to find this other birthday party i saw jamie and his girlfriend i yelled "jamie" and started to run and fell over and maddie said she heard my foot crack and i couldn't walk for two months

the punk kids at school used to wear decapitated pig heads as masks but got mad at me for spilling PBR on this girl's arm and texting this guy 'i'll fucking kill you' but he says we're ok now i saw him at the house they call the david blaine steakhouse new years eve turning into 2014 when we peed together me in the toilet him in the shower he said he hated our friends but told them he appreciated the apology he had a wolf tattoo that said beta male

on a roof sam's yelling at me to ditch manipulative men and he's looking in my eyes and saying "you have a voice"

im telling my kids i did drugs so they think im cool

everyone named david is the same

can anyone take me to hospital

my mom and dad met in the manhattan criminal courts and decided to make a tragically flawed system of their own. they fucked the first date and moved in two weeks later. im the kid you're thinking about when you look at your friend and hope they never have kids

having a kid sounds like one of those 'dont look down' moments where looking down is killing your kid

i asked my dad if he ever represented any murderers who did it and he said "oh yeah." mom took me to arraignments instead of hiring a babysitter

whenever i walk around new york with my dad he just points to buildings and says what it used to be & what year someone got murdered there

mom worked on riker's island whenever i would answer the phone there was an automated voice that'd tell me to wait while it was connecting i was seven or eight or nine and then a man's voice would come on the line and ask for mom and i said she wasn't home and mom said to hang up before the voice came on it was the prisoner's only phone call

i tried to tell her i got my period but we watched that one episode of roseanne where darleen gets her period and when darleen and roseanne got in a fight my mom said "don't you tell me like that" so i never told her

i keep trying to write about how im scared of slipping on ice or how the plant in the reception area looks dead but is just droopy or about the thirty-year-old bamboo tree i killed or how the coffee at work is worse today or about how i microwaved coffee and it exploded and i had to clean it or about how i read a book at king's county bar and they were playing bob marley but whenever i try the only thing that comes out is "everything seems fine"

after we fucked he uninvited me to his birthday

that 'one shot' eminem told me about definitely already passed and now im a secretary with an intimacy disorder

i should have used turbo tax

once i got mad at my mom for giving away my cork bulletin board and i started yelling and crying and she yelled that she gave it to a client to hang in her jail cell to hang pictures of her daughter.

cousin steve died on my birthday and i got to open presents early

this bitch reading The Secret

how am i gonna explain urban outfitters to my kids

my first kiss's mugshot is in the New York Daily News

my first crush was this kid ivan who threw up on his desk in kindergarten and the teacher made him sit in the corner and think about what he did as they threw sawdust on the vomit and left it to sit for hours

i cleaned danny's room there was vomit in the bag from three months ago and pepsi bottles full of piss on the balcony my babysitter had nine cats and called sunny delight "sunny depression." she got one eye removed and stopped saying hi. my third grade boyfriend is a juggalo now he wasn't allowed to eat red meat and i wasn't allowed to play with him anymore after he molested me

i can't believe this day is finally here. the day my dad's been dreaming about for years. we're cleaning out mom's storage facility.

he said "how did i ever live with your mother" eight times. on the way home it snowed and "fast car" came on in the u-haul and i asked him how many times he asked "how did i ever marry your mother" and he looked at his watch and said "constantly in my head for the past four hours."

does anyone have a tampon

my babysitter with one eye and nine feral cats said i'd be late to my own wedding. which implied that someone might love me one day

on vacation dad said: be careful who you have kids with because whoever you choose, you'll hate things about them, and you'll see the things you hated in your kids. but you can't divorce your kids. and if they die, well.

and then he stopped talking

can someone change my tampon. im tired

when mom was drunk she said i was gay because i kept my keys on my belt. when i asked mom if she was drunk she punched me in the chest. i tried to give her thirteen dollars in quarters but instead she said "you're going to your father's" and i said i didn't want to and she said she didn't care. and then she went to rehab

if my kids' father dies i'm going to tell them i killed him and got away with it. i'm going to tell my grandchildren that their grandfather is the only man i touched without vomiting. i'm going to tell my grandma i love her and don't have tattoos

dad says he never wanted a daughter but he's glad i can throw a baseball like a boy. dad says the dead cat he walked passed two days ago is still there. dad sent an updated pic of the dead cat in the middle of the highway with a list of meditation tape recommendations. dad says he started refilling grandpa's $5 orange juice bottle with the $2.50 generic

grandma died and dad took her deathbed for his guest bedroom

in fifth grade jovan drank country time lemonade so i drank country time lemonade. fuck that kid jovan from 5th grade

i sued my prom date on the people's court and won

maybe I'll die on a Disney cruise ship

deleting subway surfer will delete all of its data

how are people outside without murdering each other

i wish facebook had a "fake boyfriend" option

cut myself shaving

bought crackers made of rice and seeds

can't wait to try other rice/seed flavors

grab some burgers hit up the hospital switch some babies in the maternity ward

i bet my soulmate sucks

dad came in and told us to stop giggling and be respectful and that he hates Christmas and is only doing it for his parents who are about to die.

i told dad he doesn't know what it's like to celebrate christmas when your mom died on christmas

i told him he doesn't know what it's like to lose a parent and he said, "yeah i know. that's my burden"

whenever my brother and i fought as kids my dad would yell "one day i'll be dead your mother will be dead and youll only have each other."

he doesn't say that anymore

my grandpa ignored all of my questions and instead repeated "when you're old you need medicine" eight times. my grandpa says he's been depressed ever since he realized he's going to die

whenever we laughed as kids my dad yelled that he couldn't "stand the sound of our giggling."

literally show me

who doesn't like the sound of their childrens laughter

i'm on a grand central bound train and a man just walked into the bathroom and started weeping really loud for several minutes before coming out, pointing at someone's hat and saying "nice hat"

two regrets from high school: not doing drugs and not selling my drug-free piss

if i drank in high school i'd have been the "omg but do you secretly hate me?" girl at every party

but i only went to three parties

i was 'the girl who showed up two hours early'

i was 'the girl not invited to the orgy'

i was 'the girl who called the ambulance'

7-11 needs a dining area

i need more power (for evil)

The teens at the Center for Troubled Youth across the street always compliment my tattoo and my ass

what if instead of drinking liquids based on how they taste we drank based on how they felt to pee

today I Drank expired Tropicana orange juice and sent a fax At work.

here's a list of names of some people whose dicks ive sucked: steve sam sam zach jake todd jamie hank will steven chris pat geoff tim jay paul nick dan eric zack tim aaron

i fucked elliott steve sam nick jamie will matt chris pat geoff hunter mike sam jay chris tim james paul tim aaron and did that threesome that mira also had

the whole campus lost power and andy bought six cases of 40 oz and we had flashlights and when someone shined a light on the bottom of your bottle you had to chug it until they took the light away nick and i made out in the kitchen

nick's my first grade teacher ms cohn's teaching assistant at my elementary school and he says my fifth grade teacher called my dad an asshole and my mom a drunk

do roaches cum

once in this apartment i watched two hours of the kardashians and drank fourteen espresso shots.

dad drank a whole gallon of water on 9/11

does the freedom memorial remind anyone else of 9/11

im going to start lying and say i was in 9/11

my parents got divorced on 9/11

im really annoying but i wont make you make me cum

how come guys clean up their cum but never straighten out the sheets or make the bed. anyway not my problem i dont have sex anymore dad and i are both avoiding our primary care physician because he calls us fat and asks how long ago my mom died.

my internet boyfriend's either mad or dead. impossible to tell. this girl in the bathroom line said i was beautiful but then said i looked like i needed to hear it

dre took a picture of me. dre where the fuck is the picture of me. online. put the pic of me online dre

at the gas station

i'm naked in public. it's fine

texting "can you open the door i don't have my skirt"

she says we need cash and i don't know why we need cash and we keep playing the "there's gonna be good times" song from underneath the flourescent kitchen lights and the bushwick rooftops and our checking accounts haven't ever been this low except they have

i gave my friend's ex a lapdance and now that it's over i feel empty and alone. i left my clothes at the party

i cant believe i look like what i look like

a cop just said i was dark and mysterious. and hot

i dreamt someone wrote a viral think piece about how i ruined the party

everything you say is just another way to say are you my mother can you save me

i spend so much time trying to forget that i'm going to die.

im watching a food documentary but they're spending too much time replaying 9/11 footage because "obesity is a daily 9/11." i think i mentioned 9/11 too much on my last date

GEOFF I THINK IM IN A BETTER PLACE THAN WHEN WE DATED OK, IM DOING REAL GOOD NOW

i still get my dead grandma's SAG screeners

my last boyfriend didn't allow me to read (i might be embellishing here)

mom's last words were "i love you"

dad says my life made him stop believing in god

when i was in a long distance relationship i posted "kiss me thru the phone" fifteen times on his facebook two days before he broke up with me

"basic" is a term invented so the insane can feel better about the well adjusted

not caring when people die is punk: only feasible in youth

mom said her dad died but she didn't say her brother refused to take a lie detector test for their father's murder

as c hhild i made balnket forts slept on the floor and ate roaches

i ate half the apple sauce before i found the dead roach and mom yelled at me when i started to cry. i slept in a closet for fun. i enjoyed microsoft paint and aol chatrooms about boy meets world and we cried when Shawn's dad died Friday Night TGIF

i told dad i wasn't hungry but he made me eat maypo and i found twenty dead bugs in it. his forehead wrinkled and he threw out all the pasta and didn't say anything else the rest of the night

mom's last meal was a jalapeno cheddar white castle burger she threw up twenty minutes later. the doctor said she was unlearning how to swallow. a nurse said she wasn't eating because she wasn't living

dad cried

mom held my hand and i said im sorry and she said only the future matters now

cousin shawn picked me up from the columbus airport and we watched the disney channel original movie Brink!

i woke up in a cold puddle of urine to the ambulance and pretended to be asleep for four hours as they took bob away

we were picking up photos at walgreen's and i asked why grandma's namc was different and that's how i found out her last name was her husband's last name

bob died

mom raced me in the car and she won

dad says new diagnosis means i cant make fun of grandpa anymore. so from now on only punchlines about the grandpa that got murdered

knock knock

who's there

not my grandfather, who was stabbed to death on a fishing trip in 1977. his son was rumored to be involved yet refused a lie detector test

what did the mother say to her daughter

what

i wish you met my father. he wanted grandchildren more than anything. it's a shame he was stabbed to death on that fishing trip in 1977

what's black and white and red all over

a newspaper

no, my grandfather. he was a white man with black hair and was stabbed to death on a fishing trip in 1977

this guy from columbus kissed me, went to pee, came back and hit on every other girl at the bar

when i was fifteen i was sick so i asked my dad to bring back fruit and he came back with tropical skittles and an apple danish

when we opened any drawer or cabinet the dried bodies of dead roaches would fly into the air like flower petals and twist in circles as they fell back into the drawer on our silverware. you can see the indentation of where the intestines were

at my tenth birthday sleepover crystal sat on a chair in the kitchen poking the broom at the cat bowl because she liked to see the hundreds of roaches run back under the fridge

i only been to one wedding and they told me to wait in the car. we both told dad's girlfriend that her son got hurt so they would have to leave the wedding but she only yelled at me

she put a curse on me

she said she was a white witch but she was a black witch

i told my shrink "everyone has abandoned me"

thinking she would say no but instead she just nodded

my uncle tried to kill a crip because he stole his crack

dad would send me to my uncle's when he got sick of me but my uncle forgot and went on vacation we lived alone in his apartment on orange soda and imitation cheese at christmas with everyone 2004 mom said i had my uncle's chin the whole table got really quiet and no one said anything she said the bottom part of our faces were the same i think i got his nose

i guess i've seen five dead bodies

how do you know the body's dead

at least maybe five of the bodies were dead

just passed a girl in a 9/11 memorial museum hoodie

record number of people just letting me know other people talked shit about me

the woman at the door yelled at me in front of everyone and opened the door and yelled at me to go back out again and go to the front in front of everyone and everyone just saidd she was doing her job i haven't had water today

my brother drove my car for twenty minutes and changed all six radio presets

my shrink says i'm already dead

bought 7-11 water on friday. 7-11 water got recalled on monday

i skipped school on 9/11

for my birthday geoff gave me a bottle of trader joe's wine and a sippy cup with bpa. for christmas steve gave me a dog toy that squeaks when you squeeze it i bought $7 wine from 1999 and it is brown

the wikipedia for "flesh" is too short

the microsoft word paperclip reminds me of my parents divorce

i'm gonna get a paperclip tattoo because we should all strive to keep it together

does BC stand for birth control or because

this woman held a baby and this stranger came up and kissed her on the cheek so her husband started yelling so then the guy kissed his jordans

if my friend and i get pregnant at the same time but i go into labor first i'm gonna steal her baby's name

how long until 'the victoria's secret they found the dead baby in' is just 'victoria's secret' again

for my last writing assignment of film school i submit the first eleven pages of three men and a baby and no one caught it

my favorite animals are the elephant that got rejected by its mom and cried for 72 hours and the raccoon stuck on a lamp pole

hey i dont really like myself but i made this thing that i at one time liked but then, over the course of time, stopped liking because it became an accurate representation of myself, which i do not like

what if i end up being one of those mothers that hates her baby

on our date the guy that killed the rat told me he stole a baby's gravestone on the anniversary of the one year old's death

the way people talk about being able to handle anything after prison is the way i talk about middle school

every day after third grade i came home and ate a loaf of white bread dipped in red vinegar and watched the people's court

in sixth grade i bled through my pants every day of my period and wore a sweater in June to cover it up but i didn't own a coat till i was eighteen. in eighth grade Edward M spit in my hair. in seventh grade Ashanti said i'd die a virgin

i wish she was right

yesterday another one of my facebook friends had a baby while i had an anxiety attack when a boy told me he was leaving my apartment

why do crushes feel like prison

asked my horoscope what to do and it went "why even ask when you already decided u crazy bitch"

if ur not completely devoting all ur time and energy to someone you've never met before realizing u never really knew them are u even down. on the sixth anniversary of

her death i made a facebook with my dead mom's name
to message my ex

throwing up at the cemetery

i dont mean to brag but nothing matters

my friends' girlfriends like me better than my friends. i
decided not to have sex with anyone if it would risk any
friendships with their exes so now i never have sex

i definitely almost don't care when most animals die

this white girl asked what 'no chill' means. we hooked
up with the same amateur rapper

is it cheaper to have fewer teeth

i wish to never answer for my crimes

i bet people who call post collegiate life 'the real world'
havent buried a parent yet

the french call an orgasm 'the little death' which makes
casual sex 'social suicide.' i lost my virginity at sixteen to
the first leftover crack cd in a squat above the 42nd street
mcdonalds to a twenty-five year old but i didn't cum till i
was 18 with a blue vibrator

the first person i had sex with was twenty-five and rated
me on a scale of one to ten he said i was a four

what if the difference between happy and sad people
was just whether their mom came during conception or
not

April 28, 2013 1:54 PM: im looking at a dog with no eyes

my last work crush was a 5'2" fifty-five year old publicist from newark, new jersey who refused to participate in group conversation

my first kiss and my last kiss wont tell me their last names. i found out his name by looking at his subscription to Modern Cat Magazine

i broke my foot on my birthday running after my ex and his girlfriend

at the gym the 'urban warrior' trainer yelled "420 420 420" at us over a ten year old jay z song then we did squats to my ex's favorite drake track

i only date musicians and no one's ever written a song about me. jamie said he was but when he emailed it to me he said it "isn't really about any one thing anymore"

jamie was sitting in starbucks when he got hit by a car. in his bed the first time i asked what the scars were and he said he couldn't kiss me. jamie stopped texting me when his wife heard me say "i should've dated you" while they were teaching me to throw up. and because i kept texting him "i loved you"

do people ever say "i love you" before the breakup?

they put down the knives when i screamed until i couldn't breathe and mom or dad gave me water in the empty jelly jar with gonzo on the front but my throat still

literally show me

felt cut and raw and bleeding and i couldn't talk anymore dad was still in the corner in front of the windows with mom standing in front of him holding the chef's knife when he grabbed it and stepped so his shoes broke the tip and he grabbed all the other knives and broke off all their tips and now he still doesn't have any knives with any tips and when i ask him what'd happen if they stayed married he'd say they'd of killed each other

once i tried to throw my life away for the alcoholic cashier at a chain skateboard shop in the westchester mall but he was like "naahh"

is it still love if we only met twice

i woke up with a shard of glass stuck to my skin

i challenged my babysitter Jackie's scrabble word and found out what rape is

i told him the pile of glass on my bedroom floor was only from a few hours ago but it's been there three months ago

i dont think im better than anyone else i'd just rather be this fucked up than be someone else

my future self and my past self are on the same page but my current self is still texting you

this fax machine was delivered 60 days ago that's 60 consecutive days i haven't set up this fax machine anyway today is my last day i quit

i wouldn't call myself a 'life coach' but if you haven't thrown up on a dick i don't know what to tell you

i just quit my job and i cant feel any part of my body i dont even know if im moving my face right now

im the michael jordan of giving head where i once saw a dead body. swoosh

9:11 again (pm)

i metaphorically throw myself in front of oncoming trains daily and i just wish someone would finally tell me what the metaphor is

people, they tell me, "hey, your friend. he's a bad dude."

and to them, i say: "so" or "i know" or "so we gonna fuck or nah"

brie said she didn't want to talk to him at china chalet so i talked to him for five minutes not knowing who he was. the dj played a song that went "i'm shining on my ex, bitch" and i didn't dance with him because i wanted to be a good friend. six weeks later we both swiped right and i pretended not to remember and he asked why was i doing this. he said what app did you use to make your eyes sparkle and i said nothing he said i'm trying to flirt. david said to use organic peanut butter on the graham cracker and use a bowl's worth of weed and cook for 20 minutes and that i put too much. i stared at the wall and said nothing and made shapes with my hands and my coworker asked if i was dating the guy that gave me a concussion and i said it's the opposite

when i was fat and fifteen i didn't eat the whole day and danny didn't do his summer homework so he had to write the essay at the rest stop outside annapolis and i ordered pancakes and when i ate them dad said "it isn't a race" and i stopped eating and started to scream and cry

always notice when people pull out the 'best friend'

it's always "my best friend got engaged"

never never "my best friend went blind"

"my best friend can't discern delusions from reality"

my grandma picked me up from fifth grade and soaked my open wound in epsom salt. salt in the wound

we didn't have gauze so i used toilet paper and it got stuck in the cut and i had to keep yanking it out

that was the day jay z's black album came out

today I woke up to a documentary about a nun who worked with drug addicts but I only saw the part where she died

one day you wake up with a misspelled blink 182 tattoo

is it more embarrassing to want a boyfriend or to want to fuck.

i feel better after sleeping on the floor with his hoodie as a blanket. i dont care about anything designer i just want hoodies that smell like boys. i don't care about boy-friends i just want boys that smell like cigarettes

when and where can i get the essential oil 'sweaty dirty boy recently enveloped in cigarette smoke'
and some chicken nuggets

pretending my shirt reeking of cigarettes is actually like, cedar or some shit

my dad brought up his will again. says he'll send me an updated copy soon.

whenever i visit dad he walks into his bedroom and points to his second dresser drawer and says, "everything you need is in there. for when i die"

the ex im totally over showed up in my dream

ho w do i destroy phone and everything ive ever done

petition to expand the definition of crying to also mean eating and sleeping

pushing 'remind me tomorrow' on the software update that is finally dealing with my shit

waking up in the morning like 'i didnt think id make it this far'

i had sex. i cant wait to migrate from anxious back to sad

how long does it take to write a text, five hours? six?

asking for a date when a dude won't even commit to a domain name. when the whole squad like "ya man idk what to tell you"

a critical mass of "dude i just want you to be happy"s

i don't think birthdays should exist

what's it mean if u text a dude u had sex with but he only replies with "stop" or "blocked" or sometimes nothing at all?

i feel like i'm living that episode of the cartoon where everyone's trapped and we have to pull together to survive

is "sorry i was blackout i don't know what happened but i'm guessing we fucked" endearing or no

i feel personally attacked by "lol" and "ok"

three sips of red bull is giving me the 'first line i can never die lmao whos cutting the next one' high who wants to not make out with me. i said 'condom' when i meant 'tampon' anyway my period's over and he still does not want to fuck

dad pointed to the starbucks on 87th street and said that's where he sat with mom after the oncologist's and she sat and told him what she wanted and how she wanted to die and i asked if she knew she was going to die and he said it was pretty clear and i was fourteen i had been fourteen for one month and four days i sat at my desk and mom had been sober for one year eight months and twenty-five days and colleen had moved to chicago

and she came back and gave me a cd with no tracklist
and i sat and figured out which track was who and dad
called and put mom on and i said i asked they didnt find
anything right and mom didnt say anything and she said
"everything will be ok" and i said they didnt find anything did they find anything and she said "everything will
be ok" and then i ran and gave the phone to danny and
ran to mom's small bathroom where she fell three years
later alone the day after thanksgiving when she called the
ambulance and went to sloan-kettering and never got
back out i was in the bathroom and danny came in and
hugged me and i walked in circles around the block listening to "of minor prophets and their prostitute wives"
and dad pointed at the starbucks and said she knew it
then she lied to us it was in the lymph nodes and for two
years we would say she beat 4B until one day she didnt
beat it anymore

and then one day i asked her are you ok

> ---------- Forwarded message ----------
> From: Catherine Wilder
> Date: 1 October 2007 at 21:10
> Subject: am I OK question
>
> Darcie--
> Here's what is going on. The cancer is in in my
> brain in 2 places--2 spots on the menegies (that's
> the lining) 2 in the brain. They have been there
> since the Spring, and were treated with whole
> brain radiation (under the theory that where

there are 4 there are 40.) The treatment stopped their growth and no more have come. The problem is the ones on the lining. That is the "top"of the brain instead in "inside" and means it might be in the Cerebral Spinal Fluid, which means it may go other places (carried by the fluid).Those are the ones that cause the pain and the swelling. The brain itself doesn't have pain nerves so I don't feel the ones inside.

The ones on the lining cause brain swelling, and that can causes seizures, and brain death --like the brain could swell and press on the part that coordinates walking, and the person can't walk, or talk, etc., just like a stroke--its the same thing. I could suddenly lose the function of my right side, or half of my face, etc. I am having trouble walking sometimes.

A few weeks ago my brain swelled, and to avoid seizures, etc.they took the swelling down with a steroid called dexamethasone.

The swelling went down, but the drug makes me very sick. The Dr. said its sick, or seizures, so I am on the drug (sick.)

The steroid caused alot of back and muscle pain, but since I couldn't go off it, I went on heavy pain meds. They pain meds caused me to be very dizzy and loopy and woozy, and I couldn't drive, or even walk sometimes.

It also caused constipation, and I have not had a real bowl movement in 3 months. I am dealing with that now, and its not funny. I have to take the pain meds now for the cramps (narcotics for cramps!!).

There are lesions (cancer) in both lungs but they are small and growing very very slowly. The largest is about 2 cms. There are 2.5 cm'in an inch so they are not huge. The back pain is pretty much gone.

The brain radiation caused me to lose my hair, and its coming back very very slowly, and maybe won't come back, actually. Its the same as when you saw it. The wigs look better, thought, I got some stuff done to them.

I have lost 35 lb. since I couldn't eat.

The most serious thing is that the dexomethoson has attacked the muscles in the thighs in the back of both legs, and I need my arms to help me walk up stairs. The muscles in my legs are actually being "eaten" away. I cannot get up from the toilet now, I have to push on the seat with one of my hands to stand up. I cannot walk up stairs without help, I can't push my leg on the step and put the other leg up, and and go to the next step. I need to pull myself up with a banister or something, My thighs are very weak and painful. I have had several tests, and they Drs says there is no real cure for this. If it continues, I will not be able to walk, and I'll be in a wheelchair. If we can get me off the dexomthozone, the process will stop and I

literally show me

will stay like this. Sometimes some of the muscle regenerates if the drug is stopped.

There is a worse possibility, and that is that some cancers actually cause this, so stopping the steroid may not stop it.

I see a neurologist next week. Today I had chemical tests to see how much muscle disintegration I have had (roughly.)

Dr. Miller in Sloan Ketterin I think wants me to start on chemo, and the brain surgeons can target the lesions in the brain.Since I am getting such side effects from the drugs, it might make since to reduce the brain swelling with surgery rather then the dexo.

That would be done at Sloan. I will be on the job here a year next month, and eligible for disability.

What should I do about 900? Where will I live in NYC if I get this done and I have given the apartment to you?

let me know what you think.

Love, your mother

mom drove from columbus for thanksgiving we went to the diner on dyckman and she asked danny 'when are you having kids' he was eighteen. she said one year? two years?

i asked who took my mashed potatoes and i saw she had double the mashed potatoes with the perfect indent between where her mashed potatoes stopped and my mashed potatoes began

do graphic designers make typography 'about' breakups

artwork is just when people want to talk about themselves but instead of talking they give u some weird ugly object u cant do anything with

i got a pedicure and remembered seeing an amputee on the tyra banks show from a nail salon infection and then the iphone repair man said my fingerprint ID would never work again

just found out someone is very important. the guy who asked me to refrain from using the company account to tweet about cum

just found out i met my coworker for the first time four years ago at jamie's bushwick party called The Big Thing. he said, "there was just so much blood"

i cried when mom went to rehab and dad asked if i was "on the rag"

someone threw a bottle of drugs at me before my coworker recited a passage about addiction as i ate a cold egg

i ran into louis at mr kiwi and we said we were going to the big thing. jamie and his girlfriend were going to a wedding in a few hours but at the party we were drinking and conor and i were listening to jawbreaker in the living room everyone was on the roof and he said "i'm going to break the table" and i said "prove it" and he jumped on the coffee table alex has had since he was a baby and it broke and i hide the broken wood under the couch and then sam made out with me and jamie said don't make out with sam when his girlfriend is in the next room and so to get even i made out with his girlfriend and this other girl and then his girlfriend left and i went inside and conor grabbed me and i pulled away and his skull split open my chin and the lights came on and everyone ran out of the apartment and no one told his girlfriend. they're married now

i sat at urgent care but there was an hour wait so i left

two years later on alex's roof conor was on molly and a corrections officer said when he worked at the park slope movie theater he used to put salt and hot dogs in conor's soda

sometimes i want to feel like i have the conch but more often than not i want to make direct eye contact with every other two eyes and feel "you do have the conch and it is ok that you have the conch" and i will also feel "it is ok i have the conch" and "it is ok that you unfollowed me on twitter" and seeing the eyes i am directly looking into about the whole conch thing saying "i didnt mean to unfollow you on twitter" or more importantly even "i did mean to unfollow you on twitter because you have the conch and sometimes you will not have the conch no sometimes i will take the conch away from you and hold it high above your head and tell myself, 'i will never let

this person have the conch again' and that is my right"
and i will think "yes ok i know" but feel "i wish i felt
more like i thought and less like i feel" and i will feel
"ok" and i will feel "i don't even want a twitter why do
i have one" and i will think "you need to have a twitter and a facebook" and i will feel "why do i even have
this dumb old facebook people delete there's every day"
but i will think "that is not for you" and i will feel "like
not having the conch" and i will think "my brother had
asthma when we were growing up and i wanted one of
those inhalers because they were exciting because that
meant you got something special for you even if it was
bad and i will think 'people go publicly from 'in a relationship' to 'single' day in and day out' and sometimes
it feel like slow hands curling around my neck and i will
remember in 2002 when i was 12 and had shortness of
breath and was given an inhaler and don't want asthma
now and i see beatrix age 7 not liking her asthma and i
remember danny only has in from the roach infestation
of our childhood and now they have finally left my dad's
apartment has no roaches but now i have roaches but i've
gotten over my fear of them except yesterday they were so
scary and i don't ever want to accidentally eat something
that a roach touched like the apple sauce that one time"
and then sometimes instead of answering the phone hello
foxy salon i almost say hello facebook

   im doing good this is just how i sound when im doing
good. god grant me the serenity to find an outlet to
charge my phone

i m never gonna feel sad aagain I swear

wish you could OD sober

im in a van with my coworkers and the morning radio hosts are discussing suicide. i cant tell if these are sex bruises or regular 'can barely keep myself alive' bruises

another thing i did this weekend was open the front door completely naked thinking it was the bathroom. once this dude i hooked up with sent me an audio file of himself reading a love letter that his ex had written him

opening my computer after a long night of drinking alone and the horoscope compatibility website is still up

i like the eye contact that people on the phone make with people standing by who aren't on the phone

i told the last guy i had sex with that my first kiss was when i was fourteen in a second ave bar i snuck into with a thirty-three year old skateboarder who thought i was seventeen & he said "yea that makes sense"

h

imm sad again n

im punk as hell at the croissanteria

pretending not to hate my body is so exhausting

im definitely having a breakdown of sorts

wonder if my childhood traumas get jealous and bully each other

girl scouts was on the third floor of the church on 181 we didn't have badges or vests they just let us run around for an hour and walk home alone

the only sex advice my dad ever gave me was 'dont get married for it'

write sentences, give head, call it a life.

my friend with the dead mom failed the test to become a garbage man

psa to everyone on tenth ave: it looked like i was vomiting but i was just spitting out chewed up boiled egg.

you know when someone's flirting with some guy and ur like "his cum tasted ok but it gave me a tummyache"

when i was ten my dad sent me out in a blizzard for butter. everything was closed i was gone four hours but he didn't call the police

dad's jewish girlfriend never fasted but dad made us fast for yom kippur we gave up around 3 PM he tried to make brownies with raw eggs but he never turned on the oven so we stood in the kitchen eating raw batter and the next day the nurse sent me home sick

reminder that 'hey ya' is a breakup song. reminder that someone played it while breaking up with me

i wanna fall asleep on the part of the chest that goes up and down

planning texts to 'spontaneously' send boys tomorrow

terror and pain are comfortable

i have an iud but i let him buy plan b just to feel cared for. in the morning he turned over and said, "why did you let me do that"

my body is a temple in a bad neighborhood.

dude i hooked up with overheard me talking about him saying i 'lost enough dignity'

text me like i dont know how your cum tastes

does he like me how much does he like me does he like me enough does he like-me-like-me does he like me enough to be with me does he like me enough to stay with me how long does he want to stay with me does he still like me how much does he still like me does he still like me enough does he still like me enough to be with me does he still like me enough to stay with me is he staying with me how long is he staying with me does he like me anymore what doesn't he like anymore what do i do to keep him liking me does liking me mean he's staying with me how long is he staying with me are we together what does together mean how are we going to break up do you want to break up how long have you wanted to break up

i physically, emotionally, spiritually and financially can not afford another crush

my specialty is beginning to speak at the same time as a man and slowly fading out whatever im saying

someone spilled coffee on my computer and i said thank you

i wish my dying houseplant would kill my annoying cat. one hand washes the other

i tried to hook up with a corrections officer but i couldn't pretend he was funny and he owned like four guns

my shrink gave me permission to give away or kill my cat, whichever comes first. we didnt discuss the second option but it was implied

in seventh grade mom went to rehab and grandpa picked me up from school and took me to dad's but i had to go up to mom's apartment before we left and feed the prairie dog i named the prairie dog dylan i named most of our pets and the doorman had given mom the prairie dog because she liked weird animals and the prairie dog was sweet and nice and then mom told us we had to leave we couldn't live with her anymore she kicked us out and told us to live with dad but dad wasn't home he was with his girlfriend we were on cooper street in the rain with everything we could carry and no one was answering the door the intercom didn't work and we didn't have cellphones it was the second time it happened we took turns sitting in front of the building on our duffel bags and running to the pay phone to call people she had put us in a car service and we got out and no one was there after a few hours grandma answered the phone and told us to get in a cab and we sat on the couch and watched

literally show me

tv but i saw her tv guide had goodfellas highlighted and i said im sorry do you want to watch goodfellas and she said no but i knew she really wanted to watch goodfellas but couldn't because we were there and dad picked us up and i told him it would never happen again but it happened again and we didn't see mom for a week and then my uncle drove her to rehab in pennsylvania and no one at school knew except then i told alicia and she told me i shouldn't tell anyone or talk about it and no one fed the prairie dog so grandpa waited in the car while i went upstairs and mom didn't clean before she left i asked her after if she kept drinking and she said "only idiots go to rehab sober" so there was trash everywhere and dylan was jumping up my leg he was always so sweet and cuddly and i fed him and then picked him up and stood up with him in my hand in the hallway between the living room and the kitchen and he bit the palm of my hand as hard as he could he attacked me and blood gushed everywhere and he kept on biting me and i fell to the floor and threw him off of me and he hit my bedroom door that was only half a door because mom tore off the other half when she was trying to get into my room and the prairie dog came back to me and started jumping on me and trying to bite me again

id rather fuck without a condom than charge my phone off ur computer

relationship prospects like in 'a tree grows in brooklyn' when they soak stale bread to make it edible again.

i didnt take any AP classes but my mom died in high school so at least i got that out of the way

app idea: 'it could be worse' where we just gchat and i tell u about my life

a pack of rats calls up like "babe. we need to talk"
i'm like, "shit, we breaking up?
like, "i think for a little i just need some time"
like damn. how are all 4,000 of you gonna play me like that

what's a fake question i can ask instead of "can we have sex." seeing a lot of corners but can't tell which is the best to curl up and die in. i ran this far from my problems, why stop now.

imessage feature that changes the color of text bubbles for "this is a real question" VS "this is fake im just texting u cuz we've had sex"

last night i fell asleep to spotify's deep sleep playlist and had nightmares that i was a canadian skateboarder under too much peer pressure. i know a lot about the professional skateboarder rob dyrdek

hate going for a mediocre dude same way im like 'six flags wont be crowded on a wednesday' then it turns out mad girls thinking same thing

be the 'crazy ex girlfriend' you want ur ex's new girl to want to be friends with

is this a repercussion of tweeting about cum from the corporate twitter account because that was ONE TIME

would anyone like to just stand next to me making no eye contact because that somehow feels good.

difference between chill and pretending to be chill like the difference between wanting to make someone cum and wanting to have sex

i hope the internet dies today

'who up,' except 'i dont remember how to cry anymore'

i hope i get mad successful yet never find happiness

need someone new to try to have sex with

i love when bad personal decisions are also bad professional decisions.

absentmindedly confused 'throwing my life away' with 'relaxing with friends'

i love couples i just dont know where to look when i talk to them

which word processor do u wanna fuck the most, i'm textedit

i'm with a group of five friends passing around our phones to share which tweet was faved by the last person we had sex with

the only people that made me cum were steve jamie geoff hunter eric aaron

whats the difference between one bad decision and thousands of bad decisions executed every day until death? in high school i used to eat garbage for fun

game show idea: please help me im not kidding im in so much pain the longr you pretens yuo cant heaar me the worsae it gettts please where

good sex feels bad after

break ups need two weeks notice too

literally show me a healthy person

i dont remember anything from our loud drunk emotional talk but im sure everyone who moved away from us does

can't tell if i said this thing during sex or if he said it or if i just thought it. something like:
"why isnt this as good as the first time" or
"are we forever haunted by the first time when i actually came"

tell me how we fucked in the left hand path bar bathroom at a coworker's birthday party but i didn't get a concussion till later that night

grandma used to pick us up from school and take us for milkshakes i'm lactose intolerant. i went to the rite-aid on broadway and 207 and got liquid eyeliner but when i put it on my lower lid it all came off and floated on top of my eye. no one taught me how to tweeze so in seventh grade i shaved off my eyebrows

girl cannot live on "sorry how i treated u" alone

face bleeding again

any drugs that replace sex or sleep without ruining ur life?

coming up on a few friend-anniversaries. gonna throw up in their sink and ask if they really like me

is it my grandpa's birthday? doesn't matter, he stopped calling me on mine

once spent my birthday at someone else's surprise birthday party. just kidding - that happened twice

how does my cat know my face is my 'main' part

laaUghing at my pain agiain

list of things i think ive killed
baby bird
roaches
rat
prairie dog
spiders
????????????? seems like there should be more

notice no people on the list of things i killed

what if this period is just my unborn child's first prank?

new idea (for science): you don't get broken up with, you just die

my dad's name is 'dean' which is two letters away from 'dad' but only one letter away from 'dead'
it's going 2 b so annoying 2 mourn my dad ugh

whats going on with the moon and will it fix me

i accidentally offered to suck someone's dick in exchange for a pic of the moon

the moon made me feel too small so im back in bed. feeling big.

which bodily function do you identify with most, im 'vomiting'

i forgot my keys so grandma and i had to wait outside in the stairway for danny to come home from stuyvesant but then the neighbor let us wait on her couch so i used her bathroom and i was covered in blood my underwear was soaked and cold and hard and the toilet seat was stained red and no one knew i had gotten my period

the skin on the tops of my hands are splitting apart. just like my parents did. and their parents before them

'stronger to hold ur head high in spite of drunktexts than to have never drunktexted at all' is the current lie im repeating to myself

someone roofied my ranch dressing

in the unauthorized biography of britney spears she says her advice is to lift 1 lb weights and always sing in elevators every time i left to skateboard in the schoolyard

literally show me

i would sing in the elevator i would sing britney spears really loud and once the door opened and there were so many people they heard everything so i never sang again

got another building newsletter. we're no longer allowed doormats ("tripping hazard"). i don't mean to harp on this but yesterday a woman three flights up burned to death in her apartment. the building newsletter acknowledges this well-known actor for trying to save her, then compares her life to a dog's.

they quote death of a salesman. "he's a human being, and a terrible thing is happening to him. so attention must be paid. he's not to be allowed to fall in his grave like an old dog." then qualifies, "just because she was never celebrated as a 'celebrity' doesn't lessen her contributions."

mom and dad had a skunk and dad said the skunk would curl up on his feet in his sleep and he'd wake up terrified the skunk was dead but it just looked dead when she was relaxed

been stuck in the mcdonalds ball pit longer than most my relationships

would marriage exist without the concept of death

the girl who was mad at me for hitting on her boyfriend is here. i can't tell if people scream when they see me because they're excited to see me or because im already screaming.

reading up on monsters and murderers that target children like let err rip bitch im 25 now and no one wants 2 fuck

my life is like hollywood squares: where are the voices coming from. i can't see anyone. how do i get down from here.

whenever i think of those non-linear theories of time where everythings always happening at the same time i feel like fucking killing myself

there are some parts of my body that i care about more than others

a few weeks ago i thought i took penicillin but it was codeine and i posted "turnt" twelve times on the facebook event so my ex would see it

would you rather share a google doc or fuck without a condom

accidentally overbooked 'the help' (left my vanilla-scented glade plug-in on the highest level)

when i was eleven we went to grandma's in ohio and mom and dad adopted a skunk that lived in the second floor bathroom mom grew up in with the shower she was using when she was fifteen and washing her hair and her mom went in and grabbed her by the hair and pulled her out naked in front of her four brothers because she was taking too long and i was sitting on the floor with the skunk and i keep thinking "i want to kill myself" but then: "no, that can't be right" like, inaccurate

just want to let everyone know i haven't had sex since the last time i had sex and you can get broken up with without ever having dated.

wheres are all my attractive and/or mentally ill friends and/or the subway

im trying to take a selfie. it's not working. can u trust that im hot? cool people have tried to make me cum

my 'heart' is doing the thing where it feels like a runny nose

he fucked me on ketamine when i was blacked out in the bathroom before the bar was open so drunk i forgot i didn't have an iud, let him cum inside me and bought plan b in the morning

does anyone want my demons, im so sick of them
drinking plain seltzer but it tastes like vodka soda
drinking ur cum but it tastes like

nevermind

real friends spin "she's fucking crazy" into "idgi he must only like boring girls"

hope tonight ends with tears or cum

i got in the the elevator and she said:

"no husband, no boyfriend. you've got to remember, im from the generation: 58% of the men died in Vietnam. between that and the gays, not a lot of pickings.

remember the virgin birth? 2,000 years ago? we're due for another.

that woman Vivian died in the fire. burnt to a crisp. her entire body. gone. i dont know if she smoked but she was a hoarder. papers everywhere.

she was the little woman with the cane.

not today but yesterday.

you would've smelled it if you were here.

burns? all over your body? you dont recover from that.

life? after that? doesn't happen. carpe diem.

floss every day"

the elevator door closed.

two months later her dog was the dog in the most impressive dead dog memorial i've ever seen

layla and sarah were my only friends in fourth grade and the summer before sixth grade layla lived with sarah so her mom could die in the hospital and she stayed with us for a little bit i got stomach flu that year and me and layla slept in my mom's bed and when enough time had passed she would cry and i would pretend to be asleep

that kid in CCD thinking he was hot shit for knowing that heaven isn't actually in the sky, i hope he's fucking dead now. today i dehydrated myself for fun and threw up in my coworker's bag so he'd notice me i cut school by hiding between my mom's bed and the radiator and when she found me she thought i was dead and screamed real loud but she didn't make me go to school that day

when i got back from vermont dad said i smelled homeless and threw my phone against my bedroom wall and it never worked again and i went to the bathroom and turned on the shower and he asked if i was killing myself

when the skunk got spine cancer he lived in my room on the rug and his back legs stopped working but his little front claws worked so he'd drag the paralyzed lower half of his body and when i picked him up his spine would bend backwards

the coworker that fucked me in the bathroom said if my pussy was a font it'd be comic sans

i cant stop thinking of how i have to answer for my crimes on the day of reckoning.

this guy in college carried a rabbit in his backpack and he killed three rabbits that way

i want to be pelted with raw eggs

once this girl found out i was dating her ex so she liked all my vines and texted me the gun emoji asking why he commented on my facebook

im skimming this boring article to find out how many times i can take plan b before i'm irreparably fucked and broken

a healthy person

on new year's we woke up and got the first plan b of the year

the year i took four plan Bs

layla asked why we didn't have anything besides water to drink so mom started buying soda that we'd drink while going into aol chatrooms where the thirteen year olds asked us to cyber and we'd both blush and pretend we didn't know what that meant. her doberman stayed with us and scared the skunk until he died of stress

in the morning i asked him if he's clean he said, "i'm probably due for a test" and then "see you at work tomorrow"

i wonder if lesbians get called 'whore' during sex less

dad says he doesnt watch tv or movies anymore. he just makes his girlfriend watch world war two documentaries with him

dad broke up with his best friend because the rangers lost. as a kid i would ask my dad what was going to happen tomorrow and he would just say "no one knows" over and over

i peeled the NRA sticker off dad's front door. he's never shot a gun

feel endeared by the way my dad still feels burdened by the weight of responsibility for my existence

told my dad im changing gyms & he said "when i got sober & divorced ur mother i thought no one knew my pain. people have quit gyms before"

my dad won't tell grandpa he's been sleeping on his ex-wife's deathbed for two years.

jamie and i were walking to my dorm when i didn't want to date him but didn't know why but wanted to spend every day and night together and i was singing and he said "beautiful" in a way that didn't mean beautiful

after the divorce dad bought us pizza and RC cola for dinner and every night we each got our own pint of ice cream

i closed my eyes in his bedroom and told myself i'm gonna be anorexic now i have to i'm sick of this but twenty minutes later he came in and took me out for ice cream

feel like people who say 'people dont change' dont know enough people who used to do crack

my uncle refused to give my percocet bottle back as a joke but when i counted them i had to make him give me three back

my favorite sound is women older than 55 laughing

just passed crying child. good

my first human interaction of the day was when someone hit me with their car

snoopy died in mom's bed between us and she woke me up and told me snoopy died so i got out of bed and his body was in a plastic bag in the living room and i kissed the dead skunk's head

i laid on the pile and coats and posted: i want to make out in a pile of coats

i don't remember 2012

the look they give you after you tell them not to hit you when they fuck you

the last night of the lease in the east village i drank vodka and kombucha and then just vodka. i used a powertool and dre said, "now you're an artist" and i peed and shoved a tampon because i wasn't bleeding but i would be soon. we moved to the room with the big windows and i told dre he was coming thru and she said: "then switch to beer"

people talk about getting everyone they fucked all together in one room but im shooting for everyone that thought i 'knew what this was'

dad told me to write down everything i did on 9/11 but then threw away the garfield diary i wrote it in

DAD WHERE THE FUCK IS MY GOOD CHAR-LOTTE T-SHIRT

the last time our apartment was painted the painter stole my cat. i was 10 sorry for asking the office groupchat "do you think im pretty"

i took a pregnancy test at penn station once

do I want to get pregnant or do i just need more attention. you can just buy positive pregnancy tests online. zero percent chance i am but i'm still taking a pregnancy test to feel both youthful and connected

instead of a copper iud i'm just shoving fistfulls of pennies up there

i decided someone hates me with no proof again.

my ex is asking me to stop asking him "why didn't we ever date?" in front of his fiance.

nevermind found proof

my ex gave his fiance my number because she wants to hang out but now she's just setting me up. his name is edmund he works weekends

i don't think my ex's fiance wants to be friends

"it's all organized for when i die. ready" - my dad, just now, while splitting a bran muffin

the party started smelling like burning flesh

in the new year id like to have no more sex in bar bathrooms or at least remember how it started also to continue not censoring myself online

whenever i stood i threw up

'nowhere feels like home' feels like it also means 'everywhere feels like home' but it doesn't, it means nowhere feels like home

I owe everything to this golden amulet and i wish to never answer for my crimes.

what do elephants mean

i sleep next to this dead plant and this pile of broken glass

the guy who gave me a concussion told me to check out this hole-in-the-wall restaurant for their menu's fantastic graphic design. also today i woke up and my face was bleeding and i still dont know why

friends say dudes feel threatened bc i "have a stronger presence" which is a nice way to say there are lots of pictures online of me peeing

umm yea ok but has anyone yelled out ur girlfriend's name on their deathbed in the ICU

i hate the way people have a conversation and try to agree with you before you even know the subject they're talking about. i just want people that don't have anything to gain

how come everyone's ready to absolve you for your sins once you get sober but it's like you can't just be sorry and keep drinking

i gave away my cat because i didn't love her enough

I want to be stabbed

i like davids more than dans

i have to stop reading his horoscope instead of talking to him

i always enjoy proving i have friends to dudes i had sex with between one and three times. does that make sense

if i feel something it's about me. but if i say something it's suddenly about you

if i were any cured meat i'd be lox. no one starts out their night looking to get lox. if he was a drug he'd be poppers. no one devotes their life to poppers

i found out what 'shipping' means. it means you approve of someone's relationship. julia found out we hooked up and 'shipped' our relationship but he didn't

taste blood for some reason dont know why

so is the only reason we're not cannibals empathy or whatever?

i only purchase goods within a few blocks of my apartment and since i live in times square most of my debt is m&m's store related

i told my dad i have a cold and he asked if i'll visit him when he's sick in the hospital

what's the word for 'ex' but for when the relationship was all in your head you can make that ben folds song about an abortion to be about someone texting you too much just sayin

the way people talk about going home to see their parents for the holidays is the way i think about death

imagine after u die ur body gets deep-fried and dipped in ranch dressing

my favorite pastime is making people regret having sex with me using words alone

quietly remembering an inside joke i shared with someone i used to love

wonder if it's late in my life yet

air is fake

i wanna burn some books

don't worry i don't want respect

i fell on my head last night. i cant tell what time it is. seems like every or none or the color green.

my friends are talking about murdering the guy i had sex with again.

david says we can get away with it if we call it "mirder." i said my life is getting better and better every day and david said, "you're literally ruining your life right now. you're just going to get more hurt. and he seems like a bad guy"

i have a concussion from sex

imagine imagining ur wedding day

hope someone gets stabbed tonight. dont care who

someone just threatened to murder me but i had head-phones in. i said "i feel brain damaged" and then a bird shit on my head. i think im back to 'regular' from 'deeply unhappy' but probably still 'deeply troubled' and now that's 'regular'

in his defense, he didn't know how bad an idea hook-ing up with me would be. in my defense, he didn't know how bad an idea hooking up with me with me would be

everyone's horoscope says they're committing to who-ever they fell in love with on thursday see you all in hell

i didnt own a coat until i was 16

the day the president of the united states of america became an aux cord dj was the best day of my life

i am a troll psycho and i am politely requesting more power.

highlight of my gynecologist appointment was feeling the warm touch of someone who's never asked for the aux

could losing a limb strengthen my personal brand?

my neighbor saw my outfit and said my grandma was rolling in her grave. then she started yelling my dead grandma's name over and over i received paperwork that says i both have and do not have a concussion. the doctor made me declare my weight in front of the last guy i had sex with

one symptom of a concussion is being a bitch

as we left urgent care the dude that witnessed and caused my head injury suggested i was just hungover

last time i had a concussion i had a boyfriend

im going to go take a shower in the standing water that's been in my tub since wednesday

the way you have to be chill about crushes and break up before anything happens reminds me that everyone is always dead

i wake up and check nine different horoscope websites until i find one that hurts

every time it doesn't work out i think "thank god" but still only ever think "what if it doesn't work out" until it doesn't

recently i've begun closing my eyes mid-sentence, as a nice little break for both parties

horoscope compatibility says we're an idea match or at least that's what my computer said when i opened it still drunk in the morning after deleting your texts

i wish just once a doctor would tell me im as fucked up as i feel

hanging a sign in my cubicle: "it's been [zero] days since my last typo"

chin trickling blood and im thinking about everything i did wrong

oh i just remembered. this pic is from this night in like june 2014 when alex had a rooftop party for someone's birthday before she moved to la or while she was visiting from la or something and it was the first time i saw this guy who grabbed me at a party in 2012 and tried to make out with me when i didn't want to and he missed and ended up splitting my chin open and i needed stitches but never got them and no one told his girlfriend and then i decided to move to la and that party was the first time i saw him since that night and he was on molly so i drank two crazy stallions real fast and we went to the bar wreck room for the last night it was open ever and i started biting people? and i was wearing a red lip stain so everyone's arms looked like they were bleeding and then i was alone and bought a strawberita and laid in on the floor of the foyer of alex's building on the concrete on the phone with the guy from chicago who i was trying to get to fall in love with me and the guy i was dating didn't want to see me and the only thing he would text was "get home safe" while i was waiting for sam and megan and when they showed up i had to pee before getting on the subway and megan took this picture

why does my face bleed so much

have you ever walked into a crystal store and told the lady at the counter that someone died in your bedroom? you end up buying a lot of crystals

the way dudes act shitty after sex like "see, this is why id be a bad boyfriend" reminds me of the way ur not supposed to taste test rotten meat

in a lot of pain or perhaps none at all. impossible to tell anymore

i am kind and simple i wish you the best in all ur endeavors

sometimes my dad talks to me like i've never been retweeted by good charlotte

just saw a meme about a raccoon getting proposed to

u ever wake up at 5:20 AM like 'damn im sad'

my anxiety's been down since all my worst fears came true

wish i could hate my exes but i'm always just like 'yeah man i get it i don't know what you were thinking dating me either'

the coworker i fucked is giving me dating tips. he says: don't

cool thing about dating is their new girl is literally someone they liked more than you

gonna scale back on trying to be pretty. doesnt seem to 'help'

confused dog barking with whatever sound infant baby makes.

hey what's up youtubers welcome to my channel and this episode we'll be throwing out my trash for the first time in three weeks

trust women   will hook up with your boyfriend

YO YOU EVER SWALLOW SOMEONE'S CUM AND THEY WON'T LET YOU FORGET IT

dude invited me out and then asked why i "look so terrified"

how do they get the baby oil out of the baby

i havent been hugged in so long this didnt sound as sad in my head

app that can tell me if/when exes delete my nudes called "I FUCKING SEE YOU GEOFF"

what humanizes me more, tears or cum

WHAT S DIFFERENCE BETWEEN DEAD AND DYING

he apologized for not hugging me

our relationship was pretend but this break up isn't

rejection is just like any other drug in that they won't tell you what it's cut with. my horoscope says im in a healing crisis i mean opportunity.

i know my horoscope knows more than its telling me

i spoke to the cute guy for like three minutes as a form of punishment. i hope the horoscope compatibility website burns in hell

sounds nice for one person to learn and love your true self before rejecting you. i only know the dull yet persistent rejection dispersed among hundreds of people who instantaneously know they're not down

trying to calm down after receiving a text ending with a period. does a phone know it's going to die

i want to be the best amalgamation of all the girls i thought my exes wanted to date that i can be

rebranding as a virgin is going terrible

damned if you swallow, damned if you spit

the coworker i had sex with just leaned in and asked if "that smell" is me
it is

how come killing yourself is the hardest thing to do but ruining your life is the easiest

pleasse touch me

i dont wanna be in love blah blah blah

seamlessing water

listening to 'sound of clothes in a dryer' on spotify

i don't know how else to archive this but my wifi password is N7SJJHXQK4K342F3

i want to be cyberbullied by someone who loves me

in 2013 i had sex with a comedian and the story is still in his act today.

is drinking on antibiotics not allowed or "not allowed" antibiotics are ruining my life more than drinking is

im selling my belongings to afford lip injections.
for sale:
- half box popsicles from yesterday
- old meat in my freezer i forgot about
- dirt from dead potted plant
- grandma's urn

yeah bitch i eat raw eggs

boyfriends are like umbrellas. leave it in a cab for someone else

my boyfriend broke up with me here two years ago by the zine tent. the egg sandwich in my pocket is still really hot it's making me sweat. i smelled the egg scent wafting up into my nostrils while standing next to someone i had sex with

i just apologized for touching someone

i miss when i thought california could save me

nevermind i tried this pewter eyeshadow and now my life is perfect

instead of taking a moment to cry i save time by holding it all in and dispersing my sadness throughout the day while accomplishing a variety of tasks

i hate running into people when there's no natural end to the interaction so you just have to be like 'this doesnt feel good im walking away'

i know ive already said this but i'm terrified of my past

dad cancelled vacation

im the only person allowed to hate me

on my birthday dad told me his girlfriend moved in two years ago before i ate a plate of raw meat and threw up

i think 'the thing ill be reconciling the rest of my life' already happened

accidentally got a little too dark on my brother's voicemail with "im just glad you're having another birthday"

my brother is going to a funeral on his birthday his coworker was crossing the street and got hit by a bus and died. they were unpaid interns

i bet he would call me back if i wasn't his sister. if i was like, his girlfriend or his dead mom you know?

dad forgot we have different dead mothers again

i know ive already said this but i'm terrified of the future

why did my brother's ex block me on instagram. for three years. allie what happened

turns out if you fell in love in 2013 it doesn't count cuz of all the molly

im just another girl that got felt up under the neon sign in the penn station mcdonalds. someone grabbed the blind man before he walked into traffic.

things that happened in my building this year:
- string of burglaries by guy that was nice in the hallway
- fire that burned woman alive
- bedbugs
- mailman suspiciously sick for five weeks
- dead dog memorial outlasted most human tenants' memorials
- chicken spot opened
- every dog i knew died

does anyone know if i have health insurance

the weed i bought in march doesnt work anymore

should i get nachos or green juice

my friend is begging me to let him die

who in this urgent care has the wettest pussy

we met in the building across from nancy whiskey pub where mom used to take me after work where she said the owner didn't drink and there was a shuffleboard with grains of sand that got caught in the lines of my palm when i waved my hand across the wood. when he was down the block from the show he asked which door and josh let him in he smelled like the $2 soap i used to use and we talked over the band and made eye contact and laughed and i said something and he said "that's why i laughed" and i didn't say "i know" because the moment passed but when we were drunk later i said i knew and the band ended and he waited for me outside because he was anxious and i said i get it and josh texted "make him wait" and things i didn't want him to see. alex said the show sold out but put us on the list and we we walked from sixth avenue where they start calling it avenue of the americas to houston and avenue a when they start calling it essex and it would've taken the same amount of time to get a cab. todd was at the door he hadn't slept in four days and wouldn't sleep for three more and i remembered todd thinks we had sex on molly but i don't think that was molly or sex. he gave us drink tickets so i got a vodka soda he got a whiskey ginger i tipped $4 we saw two songs he drank three drinks in thirty minutes the band was a couple and when he went to get another drink i held my plastic cup in my teeth to text and didn't want him to see. he said i was from new york cause i said "deadass" and that i should talk to alex while he got another drink but alex was busy working so i texted him "i have cash if you need can i get another vodka soda" we sat on the couch and he said i thought that text said i have a crush on you but it said cash and i said yeah and he said brandon told him i had a crush on him but i didn't say brandon told me he had a crush on me and when we left i said i forgot to eat on ludlow i opened my lip to show him the matching tattoo i have with bridgid that says "crybaby" near the pizzeria that doesn't exist anymore where she dropped a slice on the floor on her birthday when i kissed the guy with a girlfriend. we didn't stop to eat and outside max fish i said i was good at keeping secrets and he said he told brandon i was cute and we each drank three more drinks and i texted bridgid from the bathroom and on the walk to pianos he said "ok i'm going to kiss you now" and then he stopped kissing me and said he was going home

we don't talk

my grocery store stopped selling kale

feminism's hard

staring at the letter k

why's the cool S not an emoji

my father, the designer of screaming cat emoji,

respecting NDAs is some nerd-ass shit

honey i have nerve damage

im at CVS trying to pull an outfit together

can't remember if i ruined my life today

i've always dreamt of moving to the big apple and starting a zazzle

turned off the debate to focus more on my own personal search for power and attention

unfortunately i have yet to find anything more funny than my own pain and suffering

i wish i was in a pot of boiling water or owned a black zip hoodie

after making out for three hours he said, "oh, btw, this is a huge conflict of interest"

why do u need scissors to open plan b

we started to have sex and he said, "i've wanted this for awhile"

i'm od'ing so the guy i like has to visit me in the hospital "so we can be together"

i always land on my feet, if landing doesn't mean success and failure is a rich tapestry

another guy that 'doesnt do relationships' got a girlfriend

i wish my exes thought about me as much as their girlfriends do

i hope someday someone stops loving me as proof that i can, for a time, be loved

it took me four days to realize the anonymous message was allie and i had four hours before the airport so we had dinner and she asked how i was and looked me in the eyes and i shook and said ok. she said before wasn't ok but now everything is ok and i met her dog and her boyfriend. on the way to the airport she said i don't have what my family has and i'm not the little sister anymore and i have to treat him like he's sick that i have to look at him like he has a flu in his brain and she said that she could see me and that i see her and she pulled up and dropped me off at the corner where i held everything i owned and cried with geoff before he dropped me off again in the same spot five months later and i thought this is the last time i'll ever see him thinking that it really couldn't be the last time i'd ever see him but that i had to think it was in case it really was the last time i ever saw him. and i cried through security in the same place i cried three years before and sat at the same gate on the same flight home in the same leather jacket and when i landed i wrote a rent check that didn't go through because of a typo

allie said "i've wanted to fight all the boys you've dated. punch them in the face. i don't want to with this one"

i texted him in the tsa line and i wasn't crying this time

leaning in to kiss he said, "am i sending you mixed signals? i'm only trying to send one"

in rehab they kept saying "the work" without explaining what it meant until we stood in a circle and i forgave a stranger for my dad's absence he held out his hands and a woman wore a veil and pretended to be my mother and i thought about what being sick means and the therapist looked at me in the eyes and we had the same eyes and she put on "the healing room" and they weren't allowed to hug me while i cried

"i have a universe inside me where i can go and spirit guides me there i can ask oh any question i get the answers if i listen i have a healing room inside me the loving healers there they feed me they make me happy with their laughter they kiss and tell me i'm their daughter i'm their daughter they say you have a little voice inside you it doesn't matter who you think you may be you're not free if you don't know me if you don't know me see i'm not the lie that lives outside you and it doesn't matter what you think you believe you're not free if you don't know me see i am the universe inside you you come to me and i will guide you and make you happy with your laughter i joy in seeing you're my daughter you're my daughter so believe you're not free if you don't know me"

feeling refreshed after dreaming i was murdered

i set fire to a bucket of salt to cleanse the spirits from my bedroom where my grandma died but the smoke alarm went off

getting used to not reading his horoscope

considering transitioning to a more fact-based reality

hi 911 he stopped texting after we had sex

im turning into my mom.... dead

game show called "that feeling is also called pain"

it doesn't get fixed it's just different problems

three of my neighbors died this week

'ok' doesn't mean anything

what's the longest amount of time you've pretended
someone cared about you. im like a year plus

any breathing chests i can lay my head to rest on?

what was i saying, i dont care anymore

note to self: khdjysbfshfsjtstjsjts